P9-CMY-420

DISCARDED

5.1
.5pts
#67741

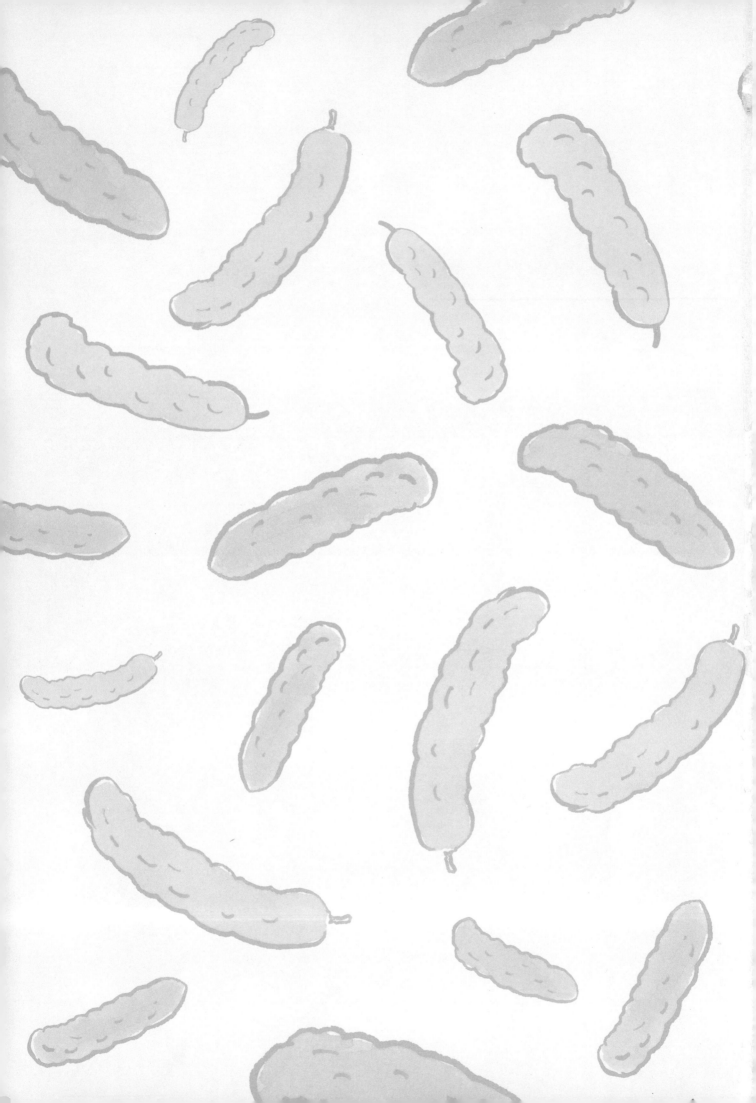

Lauren McGill's
PICKLE MUSEUM

T 25716

Jerdine Nolen

Illustrated by Debbie Tilley

SILVER WHISTLE • HARCOURT, INC.

San Diego   New York   London

Text copyright © 2003 by Jerdine Nolen
Illustrations copyright © 2003 by Debbie Tilley

All rights reserved. No part of this publication may be reproduced
or transmitted in any form or by any means, electronic or mechanical,
including photocopy, recording, or any information storage and retrieval
system, without permission in writing from the publisher.

Requests for permission to make copies of any part of the work should be mailed
to the following address: Permissions Department, Harcourt, Inc.,
6277 Sea Harbor Drive, Orlando, Florida 32887-6777.

www.HarcourtBooks.com

Silver Whistle is a trademark of Harcourt, Inc., registered in the
United States of America and/or other jurisdictions.

Library of Congress Cataloging-in-Publication Data
Nolen, Jerdine.
Lauren McGill's pickle museum/Jerdine Nolen; illustrated by Debbie Tilley.
p.   cm.
"Silver Whistle."
Summary: A class field trip to the local pickle factory puts Lauren McGill's
love of pickles to the test, until she realizes her true calling
is to create a museum dedicated to pickles.
[1. Pickles—Fiction.   2. School field trips—Fiction.]
I. Tilley, Debbie, ill.   II. Title.
PZ7.N723Lau   2003
[E]—dc21   00-9577
ISBN 0-15-202279-1

First edition
A C E G H F D B

Printed in Singapore

The illustrations in this book were done in watercolor on Waterford watercolor paper.
The display lettering was created by Debbie Tilley.
The text type was set in Galliard.
Color separations by Bright Arts Ltd., Hong Kong
Printed and bound by Tien Wah Press, Singapore
This book was printed on totally chlorine-free Enso Stora Matte paper.
Production supervision by Sandra Grebenar and Ginger Boyer
Designed by Suzanne Fridley

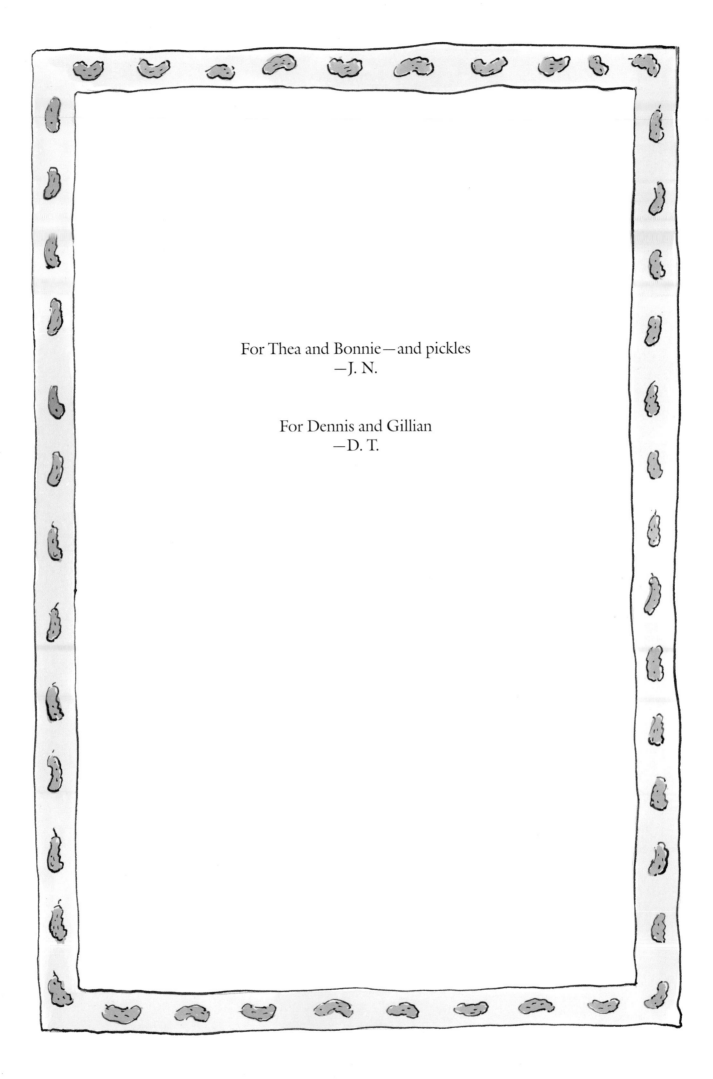

For Thea and Bonnie—and pickles
—J. N.

For Dennis and Gillian
—D. T.

LAUREN McGILL was like any other girl her age who had a favorite something. Consuela loved fried bologna. Jessica enjoyed making things. Emma loved pinwheels. Lauren was absolutely wild about pickles. She wished she had been the genius who had invented them. She wished she had been the explorer who had discovered them. "If only I had been born sooner," she lamented one Thursday afternoon. "Never mind that now. I am young, and there is still time for me to do great things. I am just glad to be living in a world at a time when there are pickles. I love them! Pickles. P-I-C-K-L-E-S."

One day Lauren decided she wanted to see how many words having to do with pickles could be made by rearranging the letters in her name— not any! But still, she loved *everything* about them. She loved their colors, and decorated her room in pickle shades and hues: glittery green, elegant emerald, chilling chartreuse, come-hither kelly, and just-jump-up-and-down jade green.

Lauren loved pickles' pungent aroma. She loved their crunch, their bite, their taste. She loved their shape and texture. She loved every bumpy, jagged, craggy, rugged, scraggy, unsmooth one. She lived to devour them. She needed pickles around her, and she felt not the least bit shy about it.

Fortunately, or unfortunately, no one else in Lauren's family shared her love for pickles. Her mother found them distasteful. Her father found them boring. Her sister found them unappetizingly ugly. Her brother, well, that was another matter entirely. He ate *anything,* and liked nothing.

Then two weeks ago, Lauren's teacher, Mrs. Munz, whom Lauren admired, announced a series of field trips to local factories to give the students an in-depth look at how things are made. So far they had been to a broom factory, a can factory, a paper factory, and a chalk factory. The children found the excursions tediously uninteresting, and said so. Repeatedly. But for each, Mrs. Munz had discovered an abundance of important facts that would come in handy on a pop quiz on the unit, Field Trips to Factories, when they were back in the classroom. The final excursion was the trip of Lauren's dreams: a tour of the pickle factory to see how pickles are made. Not a single person in the class shared Lauren's enthusiasm for the trip. Mrs. Munz's announcement was met with moans and groans.

After circling the date on her calendar in just-jump-up-and-down jade green, Lauren put her elegant emerald outfit together carefully, right down to the chilling chartreuse hat. She wanted actually to *look* like a pickle.

Lauren came prepared with jars—lots of jars—just in case samples were given. She couldn't carry nearly enough jars for all the pickles she needed, but it would have to do. Neatly and carefully, she stockpiled them in her backpack and headed off to school. It was a delightful day to go to the pickle factory. The sun was high in the sky. Her friends were by her side.

At last, Lauren thought, *things are certainly going right in my life!* But that was a bit far from the truth. The day took a rather sour turn. Just as the bus cruised down Pickle Factory Lane, a dramatic sequence began to unfold. Vatloads of pickles rained out of the sky. They pounded the bus. *Thud, thud, thud, thud, thud.* The reason: An untimely pickle experiment had gone terribly awry! Too much pepper had been added to the processing for the NEW and IMPROVED perfect-gherkin-peppered-dill. The mixture had needed to be stabilized.

The assembly line operator started sniffling and sneezing and could hold back no more. He pressed the wrong button and caused confusion in the components. All the conveyor belts accelerated to reaction propulsion speed, sending pickles flying skyward every which way and that.

The world all around was filling up with pickles. The children could not close the windows fast enough. Mrs. Munz radiocd for hclp. Thc whccls on the bus could not go round and round. Pickles lay everywhere. Piles and piles of pickles. And more pickles.

The students waded in pickles and brine. Their clothes and backpacks were drenched in pickle juice. Lauren, the only one having a great time of things, became more clear-witted when a giant and intelligent dill struck her on the head. She got a brilliant idea!

Not having been born a pickle chef or an inventor or discoverer of pickles, Lauren did the only thing she could do: Pack the pickles into jars. She would save each and every one! She went right to work.

She filled jar after jar with pickles. Then using her handy rubber lid-tightener, she twisted each lid into place. She rescued Mrs. Munz from a pile of baby gherkins. The coolest girl in class, Libby Majors, was having a very hard time. Lauren thrust a jar into her hands and showed her the best way to pack pickles, how to get more pickles per jar with *lots* of delicious briny pickle juice.

Seat by seat, row by row, Lauren helped all she came in contact with. She succeeded in creating the first field-trip pickle-packing factory on wheels. Her life had meaning. Lauren and her jars saved the day!

Out of the corner of her eye, Lauren saw Libby Majors pop a dill into her mouth. Scott and Ernest ate as many as they saved. Consuela wondered how pickles with bologna would taste. Jessica imagined pickle sculptures. Emma began thinking about pickle pinwheels. The piles of pickles had peaked and were getting smaller. The children ate pickles, enjoying every tasty, crunchy bite. Lauren watched from the sidelines as her class devoured them. Suddenly, and oddly, she had no desire to eat any. She felt cheated, wronged. Pickles had always belonged to her. Only her. Now everyone else was wild over them, too.

Later that fateful afternoon, Lauren dragged herself and her backpack off the bus. Seven steaming showers later, after emptying her mother's most expensive perfumed shampoo to get rid of the telltale vinegary smell, Lauren told her family about her day. Her father was in shock. Her mother was aghast. Her sister was bored. Her brother only asked what was for dessert. Outraged by his remark, Lauren admitted the saddest truth of all ever so quietly to herself: *This has been the worst day of my life. I have lost pickles as my very own!* She had always thought she knew how to share. But this was different.

To cheer Lauren up, the family agreed it was for the best to take interest in her pickle pursuit. Mrs. McGill planned a special treat for dessert—a delectable pickle salad. They found it so tasty, so very yummy they all had seconds and thirds—except for Lauren, who did not want any. *Funny,* she thought, *I no longer feel like devouring pickles.* After dinner Lauren went straight up to her room and went to bed.

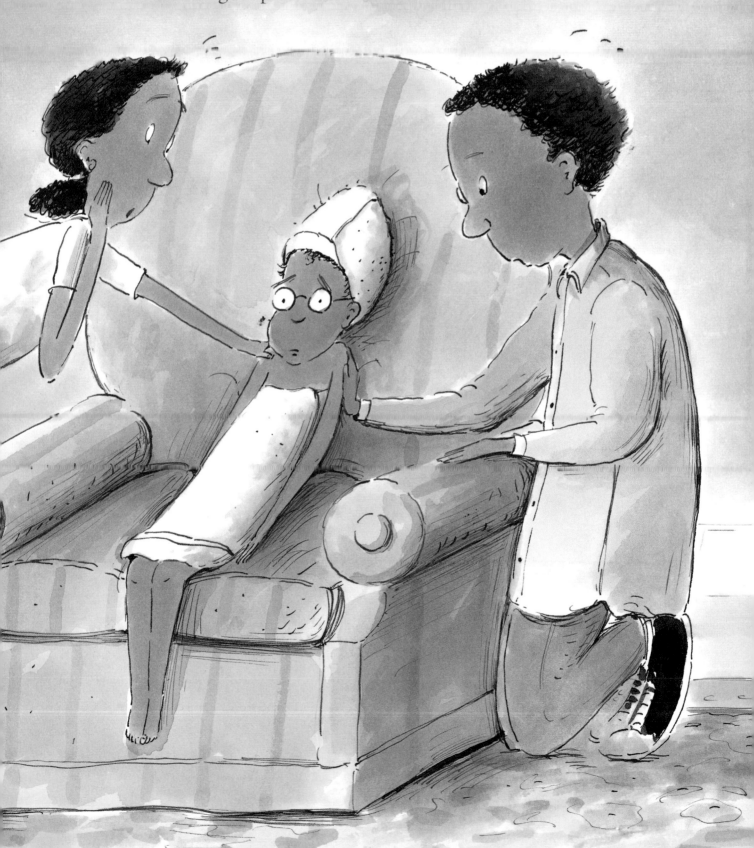

The next day, Lauren felt sick, too sick to go to school. Her mother called Mrs. Munz. All day Lauren moped around, feeling out of sorts.

Freshly laundered, Lauren's pickle outfit hung limply in her closet. To lighten her mood, she tried it on. But it no longer fit. Even the hat had shrunk. Lauren had to admit she looked nothing like a pickle. Sad and confused, she stuffed the outfit into the bottom of her drawer. She paced the floor as everything continued to turn sour around her.

At 3:00 P.M., the doorbell rang. The pickle factory president, Mr. P. G. Brine, and Mrs. Munz's class had taken another field trip. This time it was a walking field trip to visit Lauren McGill at home. They came toting a plaque, flowers, and jars of pickles. They came to honor Lauren, the person who had saved them all from disaster.

Every person from her class carried a jar of pickles labeled with his or her name on it. Mr. P. G. Brine brought along a year's supply of pickles: gifts for Lauren McGill, a memento of thanks for a girl who went into action, saving their field trip and teaching them all a most important life skill—how to pack pickles into jars! Even though the children had not seen how pickles were made, they had learned to love pickles—and that was quite enough for them— thanks to Lauren McGill. And if that wasn't enough to make Lauren a hero, Mrs. Munz announced the cancellation—no mere postpone-ment—of a surprise quiz, in Lauren's honor. Her classmates officially named her the Pickle Queen. "Hip, hip, hurrah!" they cheered.

At that moment, overwhelmed and in shock, Lauren did not feel like a queen. She felt like a sad girl. "Thank you all for this great honor," she managed to utter. While turning an almost eerie and iridescent shade of elegant emerald green, Lauren staggered up to her room. Mrs. McGill thanked everyone politely and walked them all to the door.

In honor
of
Lauren McGill
for her bravery
and ingenuity

The next day when Lauren came down to breakfast, she asked her mother *not* to make her special Saturday morning pickle omelette. And, "No," she said at lunch, she did not want leftover pickle salad. She wasn't very hungry at dinner, either, when her father placed an extra dill on her plate. She did not eat any of it; her sister did.

Lauren stared at her pickles. The sight of them left her bewildered: Who could have known that the field trip of her dreams could make her world come so undone? It was pickles that Lauren alone had loved. Her love for pickles had made her feel special. Now that everyone loved them, too, she did not feel so special anymore.

Lauren only wanted to redecorate and reorganize her room, to get rid of all the things that reminded her of pickles. *Where am I supposed to put all these things?* she wondered. "Where do *you* put the things you don't want anymore?" she asked her mother.

"Some things I hold on to, as mementos, keepsakes, and some things can be given away," her mother said gently. "Giving brings giving back."

"I have given pickles, and my class has given me their gift of pickles. And that means, *hmmm* . . . it is my turn to give again. I know, I could put my pickle things into a museum! That is what we queens and inventors and explorers do! After all, I alone *am* the Pickle Queen. And only I alone could create a Pickle Museum to put *my* pickle things in. It would be a way of giving back what was given to me!" she said solemnly.

With her parents' permission, Lauren set up the world's very first Pickle Museum in her garage—after moving her bicycle and the lawn mower. She erected a plaque in recognition of the inspiration of Mrs. Munz and her class, who made it all possible. She charged fifteen cents, the price of admission, for anyone who wanted to hear the story of *The Pickle Queen,* or *How I Saved My Class from the Pickles on the Bus and Other Wonderful Pickle Tales.*

During the tours, Lauren talked about her life with pickles. She shared her love for pickles. She showed never-before-seen diagrams of Pickle World, an amusement park she hoped to build one day, after accumulating a certain amount in admission fees.

Evergreen Forest Elementary
3025 Marvin Rd. SE
Lacey, WA 98503
(360) 412-4670

Standing amid the adoring crowd, giving out samples, Lauren admitted to herself, *Yes, indeed, I am glad to be living in a world at a time when there are pickles.*

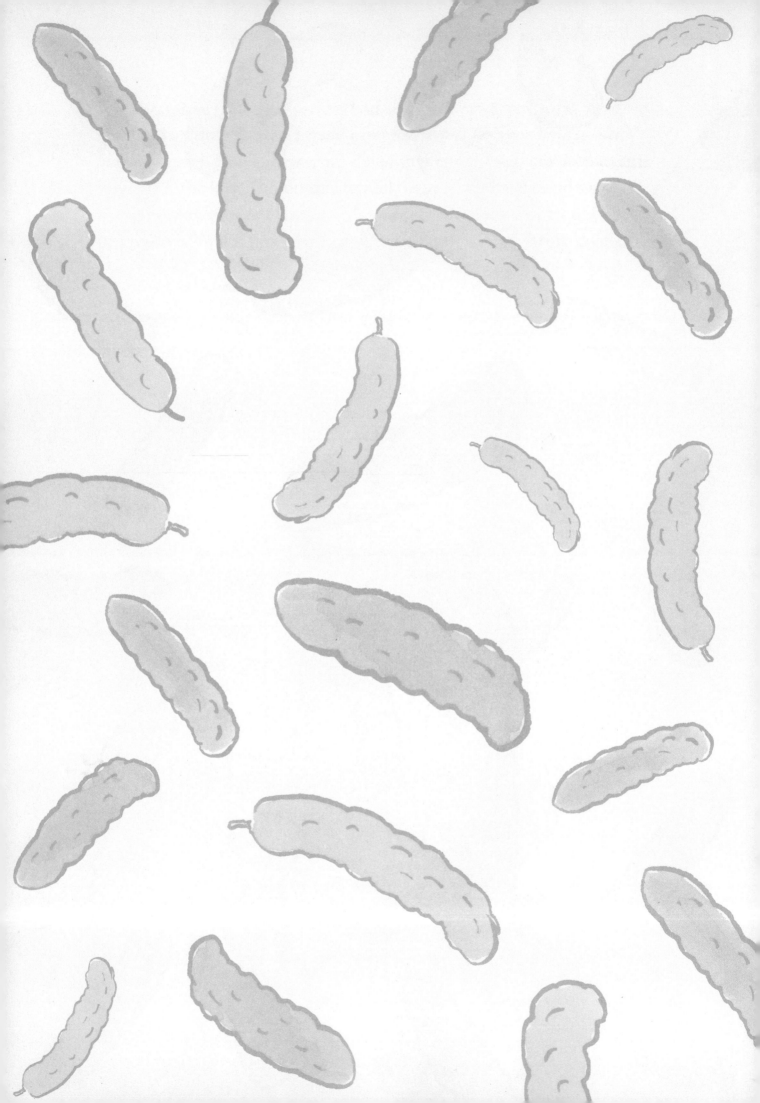